MAKE WAY FOR DUCKLINGS

DUCKLINGS

LENTIL

One Morning in Maine

BY ROBERT McCL(

D1379560

1998 Barnes & Noble Books

Printed and bound in the UNITED STATES OF AMERICA

ISBN 0-7607-1151-8

98 99 00 01 02 m 9 8 7 6 5 4 3 2 1

MAKE WAY FOR DUCKLINGS

Robert McCloskey

AWARDED

THE CALDECOTT MEDAL

AS

"The most distinguished American picture book for children"

IN THE YEAR OF ITS PUBLICATION

MAKE WAY FOR DUCKLINGS

By ROBERT McCLOSKEY

THE VIKING PRESS · NEW YORK

Mr. and Mrs. Mallard were looking for a place to live. But every time Mr. Mallard saw what looked like a nice place, Mrs. Mallard said it was no good. There were sure to be

foxes in the woods or turtles in the water, and she was
not going to raise a family where there might be foxes or
turtles. So they flew on and on.

When they got to Boston, they felt too tired to fly any further. There was a nice pond in the Public Garden, with a little island on it. "The very place to spend the night," quacked Mr. Mallard. So down they flapped.

Next morning they fished for their breakfast in the mud
at the bottom of the pond. But they didn't find much.

Just as they were getting ready to start on their way, a strange enormous bird came by. It was pushing a boat full of people, and there was a man sitting on its back. "Good morning," quacked Mr. Mallard, being polite. The big bird was too proud to answer. But the people on the boat threw peanuts into the water, so the Mallards followed them all round the pond and got another breakfast, better than the first.

"I like this place," said Mrs. Mallard as they climbed out on the bank and waddled along. "Why don't we build a nest and raise our ducklings right in this pond? There are no foxes and no turtles, and the people feed us peanuts. What could be better?"

"Good," said Mr. Mallard, delighted that at last Mrs. Mallard had found a place that suited her. But—

"Look out!" squawked Mrs. Mallard, all of a dither. "You'll get run over!" And when she got her breath she added: "*This is no place for babies, with all those horrid things rushing about. We'll have to look somewhere else.*"

So they flew over Beacon Hill and round the State
House, but there was no place there.

They looked in Louisburg Square, but
there was no water to swim in.

Then they flew over the Charles River. "This is better,"
quacked Mr. Mallard. "That island looks like a nice quiet
place, and it's only a little way from the Public Garden."
"Yes," said Mrs. Mallard, remembering the peanuts. "That
looks like just the right place to hatch ducklings."

So they chose a cozy spot among the bushes near the water and settled down to build their nest. And only just in time, for now they were beginning to molt. All their old wing feathers started to drop out, and they would not be able to fly again until the new ones grew in.

But of course they could swim, and one day they swam over to the park on the river bank, and there they met a policeman called Michael. Michael fed them peanuts, and after that the Mallards called on Michael every day.

After Mrs. Mallard had laid eight eggs in the nest she couldn't go to visit Michael any more, because she had to sit on the eggs to keep them warm. She moved off the nest only to get a drink of water, or to have her lunch, or to count the eggs and make sure they were all there.

One day the ducklings hatched out. First came Jack, then Kack, and then Lack, then Mack and Nack and Ouack and Pack and Quack. Mr. and Mrs. Mallard were bursting with pride. It was a great responsibility taking care of so many ducklings, and it kept them very busy.

One day Mr. Mallard decided he'd like to take a trip to see what the rest of the river was like, further on. So off he set. "I'll meet you in a week, in the Public Garden," he quacked over his shoulder. "Take good care of the ducklings."

"Don't you worry," said Mrs. Mallard. "I know all about bringing up children." And she did.

She taught them how to swim and dive.

She taught them to walk in a line, to come when they were called, and to keep a safe distance from bikes and scooters and other things with wheels.

When at last she felt perfectly satisfied with them, she said one morning: "Come along, children. Follow me." Before you could wink an eyelash Jack, Kack, Lack, Mack, Nack, Ouack, Pack, and Quack fell into line, just as they had been taught. Mrs. Mallard led the way into the water and they swam behind her to the opposite bank.

There they waded ashore and waddled along till they came to the highway.

Mrs. Mallard stepped out to cross the road. "Honk, honk!" went the horns on the speeding cars. "Qua-a-ack!" went Mrs. Mallard as she tumbled back again. "Quack! Quack! Quack! Quack!" went Jack, Kack, Lack, Mack, Nack,

Ouack, Pack, and Quack, just as loud as their little quackers could quack. The cars kept speeding by and honking, and Mrs. Mallard and the ducklings kept right on quack-quack-quacking.

They made such a noise that Michael came running, waving his arms and blowing his whistle.

He planted himself in the center of the road, raised one hand to stop the traffic, and then beckoned with the other, the way policemen do, for Mrs. Mallard to cross over.

As soon as Mrs. Mallard and the ducklings were safe on the other side and on their way down Mount Vernon Street, Michael rushed back to his police booth.

He called Clancy at headquarters and said: "There's a family of ducks walkin' down the street!" Clancy said: "Family of *what?*" *"Ducks!"* yelled Michael. "Send a police car, quick!"

Meanwhile Mrs. Mallard had reached the Corner Book Shop and turned into Charles Street, with Jack, Kack, Lack, Mack, Nack, Ouack, Pack, and Quack all marching in line behind her.

Everyone stared. An old lady from Beacon Hill said: "Isn't it amazing!" and the man who swept the streets said: "Well, now, ain't that nice!" and when Mrs. Mallard heard them she was so proud she tipped her nose in the air and walked along with an extra swing in her waddle.

When they came to the corner of Beacon Street there was the police car with four policemen that Clancy had sent from headquarters. The policemen held back the traffic so Mrs. Mallard and the ducklings could march across the street,

right on into the Public Garden.

Inside the gate they all turned round to say thank you to the policemen. The policemen smiled and waved good-by.

When they reached the pond and swam across to the little island, there was Mr. Mallard waiting for them, just as he had promised.

The ducklings liked the new island so much that they decided to live there. All day long they follow the swan boats and eat peanuts.

And when night falls they swim to their little island
and go to sleep.

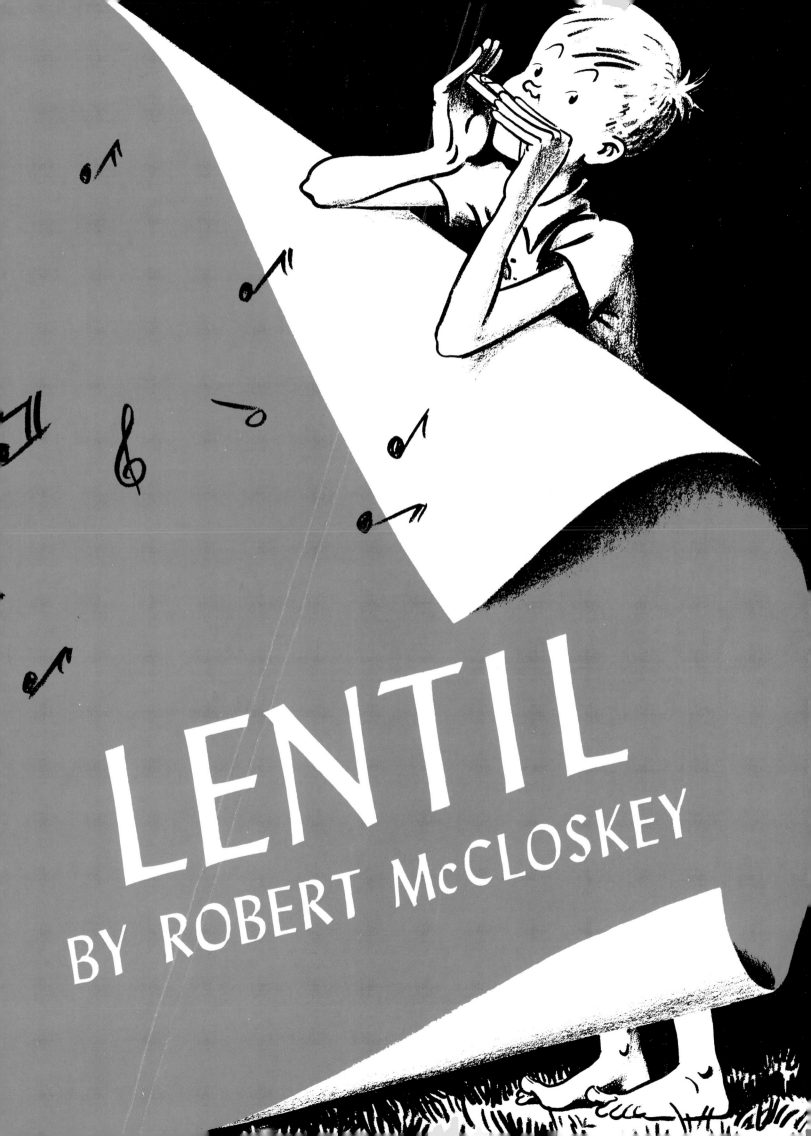

LENTIL
BY ROBERT McCLOSKEY

LENTIL

BY ROBERT McCLOSKEY

The Viking Press • New York

In the town of Alto, Ohio, there lived a boy named Lentil.

Lentil had a happy life except for one thing—he wanted to sing,
but he couldn't!

It was most embarrassing, because when he opened his mouth
to try, only strange sounds came out....

And he couldn't even whistle because he couldn't pucker his lips.

But he did want to make music, so he saved up enough pennies to buy a harmonica.

Lentil was proud of his new harmonica and he decided to become an expert. So he played a lot, whenever and wherever he could.

His favorite place to practice was in the bathtub, because there the tone was improved one hundred per cent.

He used to play almost all the way to school. Down Vine Street to the corner of Main, past the finest house in Alto, which belonged to the great Colonel Carter. Then...

past the drug store,
the barber shop, and the
Alto Library, which was a gift of
the great Colonel Carter,

SOLDIERS AND
BUILT IN
1909

by the Methodist Church, through the Carter Memorial Park, and around the Soldiers and Sailors Monument that the Colonel had built there.

Then Lentil would stuff his harmonica into his pocket and take a short cut up the alley behind the hardware store so he would not be late for school.

People would smile and wave hello to Lentil as he walked down the street, because everyone in Alto liked Lentil's music; that is, everybody but Old Sneep. Old Sneep didn't like much of anything or anybody. He just sat on a park bench and whittled and grumbled.

One day the news got around that the great Colonel Carter, who had been away for two years, was coming home. People began to plan a grand welcome, but when Old Sneep heard the news he said: "Humph! We wuz boys together. He ain't a mite better'n you or me and he needs takin' down a peg or two." Sneep just kept right on whittling, but everybody else kept right on planning. Colonel Carter was the town's most important citizen, so . . .

the people hung out flags and decorated the streets. The mayor prepared a speech, the Alto Brass Band put on their new uniforms, and the printer, the grocer, the plumber, the minister, the barber, the druggist, the ice man, the school teachers, the housewives and their husbands and their children—yes, *the whole town went to the station to welcome Colonel Carter.*

The train pulled in. The musicians in the band were waiting for the leader to signal them to play, the leader was waiting for the mayor to nod to him to start the band, and the mayor was waiting for Colonel Carter to step from his private car. All the people held their breath and waited.

Then there was a wet sound from above.

There sat Old Sneep, sucking on a lemon.

Old Sneep knew that when the musicians looked at him their mouths would pucker up so they could not play their horns. The whole band looked up at Old Sneep. The mayor gave the signal to play, but the cornetist couldn't play his cornet, the piccolo player couldn't

play his piccolo, the trombone player couldn't play his trombone, and the tuba player couldn't play his tuba, because their lips were all puckered up.

They couldn't play a single note! The musicians just stood there holding their instruments and looking up at Sneep sucking on the lemon. The leader looked helpless, the people were too surprised to move or say a thing, and the mayor wrung his hands and wore a look that said: "Can't somebody do something, please!"

As Colonel Carter stepped from his car, the only sound was the noise of Sneep's lemon.

Clouds began to gather on the colonel's brow and he said: "Hmph" in an indignant sort of way.

Of course Lentil's lips were not puckered and he knew that something had to be done. So he took out his harmonica and started to play "Comin' 'round the Mountain When She Comes."

When Lentil began to play the second chorus, Colonel Carter smiled.

Then he let out a loud chuckle and began to sing "Driving Six White Horses When She Comes."

Then everybody sang and they all marched down Main Street
behind the colonel's car.

Lentil rode with the colonel, who took a turn at the harmonica when Lentil's wind began to give out. (He said that he hadn't played one since he was a boy, but he did very well considering.)

They marched to the colonel's house and paraded through the gate and onto the front lawn. The mayor's committee served ice cream cones to all the citizens and Colonel Carter made a speech saying how happy he was about such a fine welcome and how happy he was to be home again. When he said that he was going to build a new hospital for the town of Alto, everybody was happy — even Old Sneep!

So you never can tell what will happen when you learn to play the harmonica.

One Morning in Maine

ROBERT McCLOSKEY

One Morning in Maine

BY ROBERT McCLOSKEY

THE VIKING PRESS · NEW YORK

One morning in Maine, Sal woke up. She peeked over the top of the covers. The bright sunlight made her blink, so she pulled the covers up and was just about to go back to sleep when she remembered "today is the day I am going to Buck's Harbor with my father!"

Sal pushed back the covers, hopped out of bed, put on her robe and slippers, and hurried out into the hall.

There was little Jane, just coming out of her room. Sister Jane had wiggled out of her nightie, so Sal helped her put on her robe and slippers. "You don't want to catch cold and have to stay in bed, Jane, because this morning we are going to Buck's Harbor," Sal reminded her sister.

Together they went into the bathroom to get ready for breakfast. Sal squeezed out toothpaste on sister Jane's brush and said, "Be careful, Jane, and don't get it in your hair."

Then she squeezed some toothpaste on her own brush and

when she started to brush her teeth something felt *very strange! One of her teeth felt loose!* She wiggled it with her tongue, then she wiggled it with her finger.

"Oh, dear!" thought Sal. "This *cannot* be true!"

Standing on the stool, she looked in the mirror and wiggled her tooth again. Sure enough, it was loose! You could even *see* it wiggle.

"Ma-a-a-ma!" she cried. "One of my teeth is loose! It will hurt and I'll have to stay in bed! I won't be able to eat my breakfast and go with Daddy to Buck's Harbor!" She came running down the stairs and into the kitchen.

"Why, Sal," said her mother, "that's nothing to worry about. That means that today you've become a big girl. Everybody's baby teeth get loose and come out when they grow up. A nice new bigger and better tooth will grow in when this one comes out."

"Did your baby teeth get loose and come out when you grew to be a big girl?" Sal asked her mother.

"Yes," she answered. "And then these nice large ones grew in. When Penny grew to be a big dog, his puppy teeth dropped out too."

"And will Jane's get loose too?" asked Sal.

"Yes," said her mother. "But not for a long time, not until she stops being a baby and grows up to be a big girl like you. Jane is so young that she hasn't even grown all her baby teeth yet. Now let's all go upstairs and brush our hair and get dressed for breakfast."

"It feels so different to be a big girl and have a loose tooth," said Sal, "especially when you are chewing. When is it going to come out?"

"Perhaps today, perhaps tomorrow," answered her mother. "But when your tooth does come out, you put it under your pillow and make a wish, and your wish is supposed to come true."

"I know what I'm going to wish for!" said Sal. "A nice cold choco—"

"But you mustn't tell anybody your wish, or it won't come true," cautioned her mother. "It's supposed to be a *secret* wish. Now finish your milk, Sal; then you can go out on the beach and help your father dig clams for lunch."

"I'm a big girl, and I can help him dig a lot of clams, fast," said Sal, "so we can hurry up and go to Buck's Harbor."

After breakfast, when Sal went out to help her father, she saw a fish hawk flying overhead, carrying a fish.

"I have a loose tooth!" Sal called up to the fish hawk. The fish hawk flew straight to her nest on top of a tree without answering. She was too busy feeding breakfast to her baby fish hawk.

Sal wondered for a moment if the baby fish hawk had any teeth to chew his breakfast. Then she started on down toward the beach where her father was digging clams.

When she came near to the water she saw a loon.

"I have a loose tooth!" Sal called to the loon. "And today I have started to be a big girl."

The loon didn't say anything but kept swimming in circles. Then he ducked his beak in the water and snapped out a herring. Then he swallowed it *whole*, without a single chew.

"Perhaps loons don't have teeth," thought Sal, and she was just turning to go on her way

when a seal poked his head up out of the water.

"I have a loose tooth!" Sal said to the seal, and the seal, being just as curious as most seals, swam nearer to have a good look.

"See?" said Sal, and she walked closer, right down onto the slippery seaweeds at the water's edge.

The seal swam nearer, and Sal was stooping nearer when

O-O-Oops! she slipped on the seaweed and fell kasploosh!

The seal disappeared beneath the water and the loon laughed, "Luh-hoo-hoo-hoo-hoo-hooh!"

Sal wasn't hurt a bit, so she laughed too, then she got up carefully

and started on down the shore to help her father dig clams.

She paused to watch some sea gulls having breakfast. They were dropping mussels down on a rock to crack the mussel shells, just like nuts. Then they flew down to eat the insides.

"Do sea gulls have teeth?" wondered Sal as she wiggled her own loose one with her tongue. She thought of her secret wish and smiled, then hurried down the beach to where she could see her father.

"Daddy! I have a loose tooth!" she shouted. "And when it drops out I'm going to put it under my pillow and wish a wish. You can even see it wiggle!"

Her father stopped digging clams to watch while Sal wiggled her tooth for him. "You're growing into a big girl when you get a loose tooth!" he said. "What are you going to wish for when it drops out?"

"I can't tell you that," said Sal solemnly, "because it's supposed to be a *secret* wish."

"Oh, yes, so it is," her father agreed.

"May I help you dig clams?" Sal asked.

"I'm almost finished," he replied, "but you can help if you like. First, you must take off your shoes and socks, and roll up your pants too, so that they won't get all wet and muddy."

Sal took off her shoes and socks and put them on a dry rock. She rolled up her pants and waded into the muddy gravel to help her father. He dug in the mud with his clam rake, and then they looked carefully and felt around in the muddy hole for clams.

"I found a tiny baby one!" said Sal.

"You certainly did," said her father. "But it's too small. We just keep the large ones, like this. Let's put the baby clam back in the mud so he can grow to be a big clam some day."

"He *is* such a baby clam, and I guess he *is* too small," she agreed.

"I guess he isn't even big enough to have all his baby teeth," said Sal, placing the tiny clam tenderly back in the mud.

"Clams don't have teeth," grunted her father, digging another rakeful of mud.

"Not even big clams have teeth?" asked Sal.

"Not even big clams," her father assured her.

"Do baby fish hawks and big fish hawks have teeth?" asked Sal.

"No," said her father.

"Do loons have teeth?" she asked, "and gulls?"

"No."

"Do seals have teeth?"

"Yes, they have 'em," he answered.

"And do their teeth get loose like this?" asked Sal, opening her mouth to show her loose tooth.

"O-owh!" she said with great surprise. She felt with her tongue, and she felt with her muddy fingers.

"Why it's *gone!*" she said sadly, feeling once more just to make sure. The loose tooth was really and truly gone. The salty mud from her fingers tasted bitter, and she made a bitter-tasting face that was almost a face like crying.

"Did you swallow it, Sal?" her father asked with a concerned smile.

"No." She shook her head sadly. "I was too busy asking to do any swallowing. It just dropped itself out. It's gone, and I can't put it under my pillow and make my wish come true!"

"That's too bad," her father sympathized. "But you are growing into a big girl, and big girls don't cry about a little thing like that. They wait for another tooth to come loose and make a wish on that one."

"Maybe we can find my tooth where it dropped," said Sal, hopefully feeling around in the muddy gravel where the clams live.

Sal's father helped her look, but a muddy tooth looks so much like a muddy pebble, and a muddy pebble looks so much like a muddy tooth, that they hunted and hunted without finding it.

"We'll have to stop looking and take our clams back to the house, Sal," her father said at last, "or we won't have time for the trip to the village." He washed off the clams in the clean salt water of the bay, and Sal reluctantly stopped looking and waded in to wash the mud from her feet and hands.

"I guess some clam will find my tooth and get what I wished for," said Sal. "If we come back here tomorrow and find a clam eating a chocolate ice-cream cone, why, we'll have to take it away from him and make him give my tooth back too," she said.

While Sal put on her socks and shoes her father packed seaweed around the clams to keep them moist and fresh.

"Now, let's hurry back to the house," he said, "and in a few minutes we'll be on our way to Buck's Harbor in the boat to get milk and groceries."

"Okay," Sal answered, scrambling to her feet.

She gave one last look at the muddy place where she'd lost her tooth and then started walking back along the shore with her father. She walked along slowly, looking at her feet so that her father could not see her face, in case it looked almost like crying.

"Oh! See what I've found!" she exclaimed, stooping to pick up a feather.

"It's a gull's feather," said her father, pausing for Sal to pick it up.

"Did a gull lose it? Will another feather grow in where this one dropped out?" asked Sal.

"Yes, Sal, that's right," answered her father.

"Maybe sea gulls put dropped-out feathers under their pillows and wish secret wishes," Sal suggested.

"Sea gulls don't use pillows, but I suppose they can make wishes," her father said.

"Then I'll make my wish on this *feather*," Sal decided.

"Perhaps the sea gull has already made a wish on that feather and the wish is used up," suggested her father.

"Oh, no," Sal said definitely, "he didn't, you see. I guess because he was too busy flying and not looking back. He didn't notice it was loose when he brushed his feathers this morning, so he didn't expect it would drop out. He doesn't even know it's gone," she convinced herself. She closed her eyes tight and wished her secret wish.

When they reached home Sal's mother and sister Jane
were waiting with a box of empty milk bottles to return to
the store and a list of things to buy.

"I'll have a nice clam chowder ready for your lunch when
you get back," said Sal's mother, waving good-by.

"I'll take good care of Jane," Sal promised. "I'm a big girl
and I can watch so she doesn't tumble into the water."

Sal and Jane and their father went down to the shore
and got aboard their boat.

Sal and Jane put on their life preservers while their father prepared to start the outboard motor. He pulled and he pulled on the rope to start it, but the outboard motor just coughed and sputtered and wouldn't start.

So he had to row the boat all the way across the bay to
Buck's Harbor where the store was.

The harbor was full of boats, and Sal's father rowed their boat among them, up to a landing, and tied it so it would not drift away while they were at the store. They all climbed ashore, and Sal's father brought along the milk bottles. He brought the outboard motor too, so Mr. Condon who ran the garage could fix it.

As they came up the path to the village Mr. Condon was outside his garage, putting gas into a car.

"I have a tooth out!" Sal greeted. "And our outboard motor won't run."

"My, such trouble!" Mr. Condon commented, and after he had admired the empty place where Sal's tooth was missing

they took the outboard motor into the garage to find why it wouldn't run. Mr. Condon pinched a little with his pliers, tunked a bit with his hammer, and then, after selecting a large wrench, he took out the spark plug.

"Came right out, just like that tooth of yours, didn't it, Sal?" he said, holding it up to the light. "Humph!" he grunted, tossing it on the floor. "Needs a new plug!"

Sal was just about to ask how long it would take for a new spark plug to grow in when Mr. Condon reached up on the shelf

and picked out a brand-new one, and put it in the motor.

Sal picked up the old spark plug and handed it to sister Jane. Jane was so little that she didn't understand about secret wishes. Jane was so little that she couldn't even say ice-cream cone! So Sal wished the secret wish for Jane on the spark plug.

Mr. Condon pulled the rope, and the motor started right up, just as good as new. Sal's father thanked him and picked

up the motor and the milk bottles. Jane carried her spark plug, Sal carried her feather, and they said good-by and walked across the street to where Mr. Condon's brother kept store.

"Well, look who's here!" said the Mr. Condon who kept store.

"I have a tooth out!" Sal shouted, returning Mr. Condon's greeting.

She showed the empty place where her tooth had been, first to Mr. Condon, then to Mr. Ferd Clifford and Mr. Oscar Staples, who were sitting in the store talking about trapping lobsters and how the fish were biting.

"Don't put your tongue in the empty place," Mr. Clifford advised, "and a nice shiny gold one like mine will grow in."

"But I didn't know soon enough," said Sal, looking confused.

"Hawh!" said Mr. Condon, chuckling. "Don't you go worry-in' about everything these jokers suggest. I don't suppose," he added, opening up his freezer, "that you could eat an ice-cream cone with one of your teeth out?"

"Oh, yes, I could!" said Sal. "And it's supposed to be chocolate!"

"And this little lady?" he questioned, turning to Jane.

"Hers is supposed to be vanilla, so the drips won't spot, and you'd better push it together tight, so it won't drop off," Sal dictated, "because she's still almost a baby and doesn't even have all of her first teeth."

After Mr. Condon had put the groceries and milk in the box, they thanked him once more and waved good-by. They walked down the path to the harbor

and down the runway to the float where their boat was tied. They all climbed aboard, carrying the outboard motor, the box of milk and groceries, the feather, the spark plug, and the ice-cream cones.

While their father fastened the outboard motor to the boat Sal and Jane finished their ice-cream cones.

"I want s'more!" Jane demanded.

"Silly!" exclaimed Sal. "Our wishes are all used up." Then she remembered that she was growing up, and just like a grownup she said, "Besides, Jane, two ice-cream cones would ruin your appetite. When we get home we're going to have

CLAM CHOWDER FOR LUNCH!"